OOM RAZOOM

OR GO I KNOW NOT WHERE, BRING BACK I KNOW NOT WHAT

· A RUSSIAN TALE ·

RETOLD BY
DIANE WOLKSTEIN

ILLUSTRATED BY
DENNIS McDERMOTT

MORROW JUNIOR BOOKS
NEW YORK

Oil glaze was used for the full-color artwork. The text
type is 14 point Novarese Book.

Text copyright © 1991 by Diane Wolkstein
Illustrations copyright © 1991 by Dennis McDermott
Inquiries should be addressed to
William Morrow and Company, Inc.,
1350 Avenue of the Americas,
New York, N.Y. 10019.

Printed in the United States of America.
1 2 3 4 5 6 7 8 9 10
Library of Congress Cataloging-in-Publication Data
Wolkstein, Diane.
Oom razoom, or, Go I know not where, bring back I know not what:
a Russian tale/retold by Diane Wolkstein;
illustrated by Dennis McDermott.
p.   cm.
Summary: A retelling of an old Russian tale of Alexis the king's
archer, his beautiful and magical wife Olga, and their adventures.
ISBN 0-688-09416-3.—ISBN 0-688-09417-1 (lib. bdg.)
[1. Fairy tales. 2. Folklore—Soviet Union.] I. McDermott,
Dennis, ill.   II. Title.   III. Title: Go I know not where, bring
back I know not what.
PZ8.W8160o   1991
[398.21]—dc20   91-6308   CIP   AC

To Olivier Bernier
—D.W.

For Dan and Chris
—D. McD.

"The morning is wiser than the evening."
That's what the archer's wife says.
Alexis met his wife in the woods. I'll tell you how.

One morning Alexis, the king's archer, went into the woods to kill birds for the king's dinner. When he raised his bow to shoot a certain blue pigeon, she cried out, "Do not harm me. I will bring you good fortune."

"A bird who speaks," Alexis marveled. "I will certainly not kill such a wonder."

He brought her home and put her on his windowsill. She tucked her head under her wing as if she would sleep, then fell to the ground and turned into a beautiful young woman—the most beautiful woman you or I have ever seen.

"You have won my heart," she said, "and I choose you as my husband. If you choose me as your wife, you must learn the secret of my heart."

"I choose you," he said, and they married at once. The next day Alexis returned to his duties as archer for the king.

They lived together happily, but the young wife, Olga, worried for her husband, who came home every evening weary and wet from tramping through the marshes. One evening she said, "My dear husband, let us try another way to earn our bread. Bring me two hundred rubles' worth of silk thread, and I will weave a beautiful carpet for you to sell."

Alexis believed in his wife. So he borrowed ten rubles from one friend and twenty from another until he had two hundred rubles. When he brought her the thread, she said to him, "Husband, be of good cheer, trust in God, go to sleep. The morning is wiser than the evening."

In the morning, on the ground outside their house, there was a carpet on which all the kingdom was embroidered: the palace, the villages, the rivers, the lakes, and even their little hut. "Sell the carpet to the merchants in the market," Olga said, "and take whatever price they offer you."

Alexis carried the carpet to market. The first merchant he met admired the carpet and wanted to buy it.

"What is your price?" he asked.

"You are a merchant, you set the price," Alexis replied.

The merchant thought and thought and could not think of a price for such a marvelous carpet. And so it went all day. Many traders wanted the carpet, but no one could set a price.

It happened that the king was passing the marketplace. When he saw the large crowd, he ordered his carriage to stop and his steward to find out what was for sale. The steward returned with the carpet.

"What price?" the king asked.

"The price is not known," the steward replied. "The archer's wife, who made it, said he is to accept whatever is offered."

"Ten thousand rubles!" the king said at once.

The archer accepted the rubles happily, and the king returned to the palace with the carpet.

At first the carpet hung in the hall. But the king so delighted in it that he brought it into his bedroom.

One morning he decided he wanted to meet the woman who had woven the carpet, so he set off in disguise. The archer was away when the king entered the

simple hut. He stared at Olga. He stared and stared. Never had he seen such beauty, never on earth. But she belonged to another man. Well, that could be fixed, the king thought. Quickly he left the hut, turning his head as he walked out so he could keep her beauty in his mind as long as possible.

That evening the king sent his steward into the back alleys to look for Baba Yaga, the witch. Baba Yaga appeared and hissed, "*Shahahh! Shahahhhh!*" And all of her chins began to bobble.

The steward said, "Help me, grandmother, and I'll pay you whatever you wish. The king wants to rid the kingdom of the archer Alexis—"

"A*hhh*, he's an easy one, but his wife—she's the cunning one. Yessss!" Baba Yaga hissed and her tongue went out with each breath. "*Shahahh*. But I'll tell you the way! Send the archer I Know Not Where and have him bring back I Know Not What. H*ah-hah-hah*! He'll be gone *forever*!"

The next evening the archer came home to his wife with his head on his chest.

"My beautiful Olga," he said, "the king wishes me to go on a mission for him. I am to go I Know Not Where and to bring back I Know Not What. Now, good wife, tell me, how in the world is a person to do that?"

"Yes," Olga agreed. "This is a difficult task. It will take nine years to get there and nine years to return. But do not grieve, be of good cheer, trust in God, go to sleep. The morning is wiser than the evening."

The next morning Olga gave him a handkerchief and a ball. "Follow the ball wherever it rolls," she advised him. "And do not use any handkerchief but this."

The king gave Alexis gold. The cannons saluted. Alexis bowed low to the four directions and went out the city gates. He threw the ball and followed it as it rolled.

The very next day, Olga was brought to the palace. She was led into a golden room, where the king happily welcomed her.

"Good day, beautiful woman," the king said. "Your husband is gone, and, as you well know, he may never return. If you wish to be queen, I will marry you."

"I have never heard of a woman marrying another man when her husband is alive."

"Then you refuse. Well, I shall take you by force."

The king reached out for her, but the young woman just smiled. She fell to the floor, turned into a blue pigeon, and flew out the open window.

The ball rolled over land and sea, and Alexis followed. When the ball came to a river, it opened up into a boat; and when the archer was tired, it spread out and became a downy bed.

On the ball rolled until it came to a palace and disappeared up a flight of steps. Three lovely girls appeared and brought Alexis food and drink and a bowl to wash in. He refused the towel they offered, explaining that he had his wife's handkerchief. But when he pulled out her handkerchief, the girls cried in amazement, "Look! That's our sister Olga's embroidery."

They called their mother. The archer told them of his wife and his mission to go I Know Not Where and bring back I Know Not What.

"My dear son-in-law, this is a marvel that even I do not know. But I will call my helpers." And she went out on the porch and called to the animals of the land and the birds of the air. But they all answered in one voice, "No, we do not know how to go I Know Not Where and bring back I Know Not What."

Then his wife's mother called to her giant helpers to take her to the middle of the ocean, and there she called to the fish and reptiles of the sea. But they all answered in one voice, "No, we do not know how to go I Know Not Where and bring back I Know Not What."

Just then an old frog croaked, "Qwaa—qwaa! I know. It is at the end of the world. I would take him, but I am so old I would not get there in fifty years."

In a trice they were at the palace. Olga's mother put the frog in a jar of fresh milk, gave the jar to Alexis, and said, "Let the frog lead you."

The frog spoke, and Alexis obeyed. On and on they went. Was their journey long? you ask. Was it short? Well, it was as long and as short as it takes a tale to be told.

"*Qwaa!*" croaked the frog. "We are here." Alexis looked and saw a river of fire.

"Take me out and sit on me!" the frog ordered, but the archer didn't want to crush the little frog.

"Spare me not," the frog insisted. So Alexis sat on the frog. As he did so, the frog began to swell, larger and larger, until she leaped with the archer on her back across the river of fire and landed on the other side of the river in front of a door leading into a mountain cave.

"Go into the cave and hide," said the frog. "Two men will come in. Watch what they do, and after they leave the cave, do the same. I will wait for you."

The archer's heart beat loudly as he entered the dark cave and groped about. He found an empty cupboard and hid inside it. Then he heard voices. Two men came in and shouted, "*Oom Razoom*! Bring food! *Oom Razoom*! Bring drink!"

At once a table appeared with brightly lit candles and plates piled high with delicious food. The men ate and drank and then shouted, "*Oom Razoom*! Clear it away!" Everything disappeared, the light went out, and the men were gone.

Alexis waited. Then he came out of the cupboard and shouted, "*Oom Razoom*! Bring food! *Oom Razoom*! Bring drink!" And again a table appeared with brightly lit candles and plates piled high with delicious food. But Alexis said, "Oom Razoom, are you hungry? Do you want to eat with me?"

"My precious man," a voice said. "Where do you come from? For thirty years I have served those two, and they have never once invited me to sit with them and eat."

Alexis did not see anyone, but he watched as the enormous pile of food and drink began to disappear. Yet each time the plates and glasses emptied, they were filled again.

After they had eaten, Alexis said, "Oom Razoom, are you not tired of this dusty cave? Would you not like to come with me and be my servant? I will treat you well."

"Why not? You are a kind man. Thirty years in a dusty cave is enough. I will follow you."

They left the cave. Alexis sat down on the frog, and, in a trice, they were back at the palace. Oom Razoom prepared wonderful dishes for everyone. And Olga's mother declared that the old frog should have a full glass of milk every day for her services.

Then the archer and Oom Razoom set out for home.

The archer walked and walked, on and on. Was his journey long? you ask. Was it short? Well, this time I think it was a little long, for he began to sigh, "Ah me, ah me, my legs are dropping off."

"Well, why didn't you say so before?" a voice said. In a trice, a breeze lifted Alexis into the air. "Stop!" he cried. "My cap has fallen off."

"Too late," Oom Razoom said. "Your cap is now two thousand versts away. But look, we are over the sea. If you wish, I will make you an island. There you can rest, and from those who come to visit, you can earn what you need."

As they descended, Oom Razoom advised Alexis, "Three ships will stop at your island. Sell me for whatever the ships' captains suggest. And I will return when you wish."

Soon, just as Oom Razoom had said, three merchant ships arrived. "What a marvel," the captains said. "We have sailed this way many times, but we have never seen this island before."

Alexis welcomed the captains and invited them to rest and to feast. They all sat down under an arbor. Alexis commanded, "*Oom Razoom*! Bring food! *Oom Razoom*! Bring drink!" At once a table appeared, piled high with the captains' favorite foods.

"What a marvel!" they cried. "We must make an exchange."

The first captain took a little box from his pocket, opened it, and a splendid garden filled with exquisite flowers and trees and a flowing stream covered all the island. He closed the box and the garden disappeared.

Then the second captain took an ax from his pants, struck a stone, and *rap-tap*, there was a ship. *Rap-tap*, there was another ship. He struck one hundred times and one hundred ships with sails and guns and sailors stood waiting for orders. Then the captain put away his ax and everything disappeared.

The third captain took out a horn, blew it, and an army with flags and cannons and soldiers began to march. When the noise became too loud, the captain blew into the other end of the horn and everything disappeared.

"Well, that is fine," said Alexis, "but see how peacefully I live. What use do I have for such things?" But the captains, thinking that with such a servant they could live the rest of their lives without care, insisted.

"Ah me, ah me, if you so insist," said Alexis. "But I will only exchange my servant for all three marvels."

"Agreed!" the captains said, and they shouted, "*Oom Razoom*! Bring food! *Oom Razoom*! Bring drink!" And the captains ate and drank so much they soon fell asleep.

Alexis sat alone in his arbor. "I do miss Oom Razoom," he sighed.

"You do?" a voice said. "Well, here I am. What is your wish?"

"I am ready to go home," Alexis replied. And in a trice, a breeze lifted him into the air, and he was on his way home.

As they descended, Alexis asked Oom Razoom, "Could you possibly build a
castle for me?"

"Why, of course."

And when they reached the earth, a castle was waiting for Alexis. He opened
his box and a beautiful garden with trees and flowers and bushes and a flowing
stream covered the land. Alexis sat in his castle enjoying the view. He sat there

all day looking from tree to flower to bush, watching and waiting. At sunset, a blue pigeon flew in the open window, fell to the floor, and turned into his wife.

Did they hug? you ask. Did they kiss? Oh, yes. And then they told tales all night, for eighteen years had passed, eighteen years, long and short, filled with many adventures.

The next morning, from his balcony, the king blinked his eyes. He blinked and blinked, but the castle facing his palace did not disappear.

The king was furious. "Who dares to build a castle in my kingdom without my permission?"

When his messengers returned with word that the castle belonged to the archer and he was living there happily with his wife, the king was even more furious. He trembled with rage and ordered his army to destroy the castle, to cut down the garden, and to kill the archer and his wife.

Alexis saw a great army marching toward him. He took out his ax. *Rap-tap*. A ship appeared. *Rap-tap*. Another ship. He struck one hundred times and one

hundred ships with sails and guns and sailors were ready. He blew his horn, and an army with flags and cannons and soldiers awaited his orders.

"Begin battle!" Alexis cried.

Then the drums beat. The horns blew. The cannons fired. The flags waved. And the soldiers marched forward. Within an hour, the king's army began to flee. The king tried to stop them but was killed in the retreat. After the king was killed, the army returned. The people gathered together and asked Alexis to rule their kingdom.

"It will soon be dark," the archer said. "I will let you know in the morning. The morning is wiser than the evening."

Did he become king? you ask. Did he rule wisely? Oh, yes, with the help of his wife, Olga, very wisely. As for Oom Razoom, he is retired and living peacefully. And so may it be for all of us.

j398.2   Wolkstein, Diane
WOL
            Oom razoom, or, go I
            know not where,
            bring back I know
            not what

$14.95   50319

DATE			
SEP 28 1991			
JUL 23 1992			
APR 18 1994			
JUL 13 1994			
APR 28 1995			
FEB 11 1999			